Introduction

Step into a world where the ethereal and the macabre intertwine, where beauty and darkness collide and the essence of the human experience is at its most primal. "Angels & Nightmares: Volume 3," the third installment of a series that delves deep into the complexities of creative writing and poetry twist the imagination.

With profound introspection and evocative language, these verses lay bare the conflicts that plague us, the transformative journeys we undertake and the inherent suffering that endures with all living beings.

As we delve deeper into "Angels & Nightmares: Volume 3," you will find that it goes beyond the exploration of personal turmoil. It dares to confront the harsh reality of existence, where the strong is a driving force that shapes the evolution of life. From the tiniest microcosms to the grandeur of the natural world, the emphasis on adaptation, resilience and the pursuit of survival permeates these stories.

Let the tales and rhythmic poems transport you in a world where angels and nightmares coexist, where conflict and violent changes bind and the survival of the fearless becomes an undeniable reality.

"Angels & Nightmares: Volume 3" is an invitation to confront suffering head-on and to discover the extraordinary resilience that resides within each and every one of us.

Contents

"In the bustling streets filled with rushing bodies and indifferent faces, a small and fragile creature navigated its way through the chaos. A homeless man abandoned by the world, walking unnoticed amidst the lives of those who passed by. With each step, he yearned for warmth and compassion, but all he received was neglect and indifference.

"As weeks turned into years, a strange phenomenon began to unfold within him. When averted away from his presence, he could feel a rapid change stirring within. It was as if his physiology responded to the emotional distance of those who refused to acknowledge his existence.

"Confusion clouded his innocent eyes. He didn't understand the reason behind this transformation or what it was changing into. Fear mingled with curiosity and an unspoken desire to belong emerged within his fragile heart. But the world around it remained oblivious, wrapped up in their own lives, unaware of the extraordinary journey unfolding within."

These urban bustling scape,
I wander along denied.
Wander through rushing chaos,
Needing to belong rather than hide.

Ignored by ongoing passersby,
Their view turned a blind eye.
Affording time opposed to rectify,
No one knew kindness inside.

Everyone for themselves,
But a shift occurs automatic.
Physiology ever altering,
Unknown to the world, can't stand it.

From miniscule form, I expand,
Dramatically drastic.
Raw but now formless,
I'm lost and dizzy like an addict.

Fate had other plans,
Transformation continues messy.
Bizarre with softness of fur,
My form now brand new and ready.

Wings push open, bursh etching,
Leaping for the cityscape.
Seeking solace and acceptance,
From the gazing eyes of hate.

Still incomplete, a yearning deep within,
Gaze at my pathetic state.
Until I reach the ocean's shores,
Where my journey began centuries late.

As the waves crash upon the sand,
a miracle took place.
My bird brain transforms,
Into a creature full of grace.

Turn back, jurassic emerges,
With scales and ancient weight.
A symbol of resilience,
Transformation at an impressive rate.

With joy and newfound freedom,
I plunge into the deep blue,
Swimming through the waters,
Where only dreams come true.

No longer ignored or cast aside,
Found my rightful place anew,
A creature of the vast waters,
I smile upon comfort, the primal sea will do.

The Red Hunt

"In the heart of a bamboo-laden realm, amidst the tranquil beauty of nature, we find a courageous creature known as Tam, a Red Panda facing an extraordinary test of survival. A creature of delicate grace and vibrant red fur, roams freely through her bamboo-dense home. From the depths of the darkness unknown, a pack of fearsome white tiger dragons emerge, their predatory eyes lock onto their red prey.

"With lightning powerful speed, the assault begins. The tiger dragons surround Tam, their numbers overwhelming, their ferocity unmatched. She finds herself thrust into a terrifying dance of survival, leaping and scrambling through the labyrinthine trees and shimmering ponds, a desperate attempt to evade the relentless pursuit.

"In this parallel dimension, Tam becomes the hunted, her once peaceful home transformed into an arena of peril. Her agility and resourcefulness are put to the ultimate test as she battles against insurmountable odds, a solitary figure against a malevolent force."

She ventured further,
Through the dizzying maze and grime.
Each dragon swept her,
Cunning oblivion ways to climb,

Trapping the bear fast,
Her fate turned and entwined.
Cracking awareness surpassed,
Making a demise better timed.

Then one by one,
Traps violently spawned.
Tam coming undone,
Traps silently called.

The white tiger dragons,
Though fierce and broad.
Fighting tirelessly the assassin,
Their efforts appalled.

Through the gaping dark,
Tam weaved her quickness ways.
Doomed escaping jaws,
Dragons ran, they're now the prey.

Her paws propelled increasingly,
Like a darting loud flame.
Dragon ranks delved seemingly,
They started proud, now in shame.

At last of the hunt,
Tam stood victorious.
The bamboo haven front,
Lessons for food notorious.

Feasting on the meat and spoils,
Her trophies taste of grand,
The white tiger dragons recoiled,
Now conquered, devoured and damned.

Tam the Red Panda,
Boldly empowered to stand,
A symbol of courage at random,
Countered the hunt as planned.

The Egghead Lady

"A seemingly ordinary elementary school, nestled within the confines of a modern town. Behind its innocent facade, there lies a twisted secret, a spectral enigma that has plagued decades of young students who dared occupy the boys' bathroom. This is the haunting tale of The Egghead Lady.

"Through time, skepticism took hold. No tangible evidence could be found to substantiate these outrageous claims. Doubt remained in the air as a myth, leaving the existence of The Egghead Lady relegated to the realm of urban legend. Whispers of the phantom suggested that she only haunted when visitors entered the bathroom alone

"On a fateful day, brought forth a 10 year old boy named Corey, whose path would intertwine with this phenomenon. It was in the solemn solitude of that boys' bathroom that Corey encountered her presence. The lights dimmed so slightly as the exit door seemed to grow further away. From the mist of darkness, she materialized."

Decades of haunting,
She appeared like death.
The boys bathroom stalking,
Where she scared and kept,

All the little boys talking,
Corey didn't believe and went.
Kids avoided and flocking,
Same fear to accept.

Floating above dirty ground,
The Egghead Lady a ghastly sight.
Choking from buried sounds,
A scream of crazy hands of nasty ice,

Corey shivered his head down,
His courage struggled with nervous height,
Yet deep within his glare down,
Strength remained observed and precise.

His nerves shook in horror,
But he stood his shaken ground.
The cold chaos less warmer,
His mood stayed profound,

The Egghead Lady warning,
Her fear unveiled booming sound.
Witnessing the boy's courageous form,
His body stationed and about.

With a gasp and a bleak shudder,
She backed down and transformed.
From monstrous fiending world of another,
To a figure sound and warm,

A gentle sweet old lady,
Soft, kind and reformed.
Her haunting nature left behind,
Her smile soothed and adored.

Fading away in a shimmering gas,
She whispered words that will forever last,

*"Fear fades when faced, my dear young lad,
Stand tall and brave, it's not so bad."*

Corey uncovered and enlightened,
Learned a powerful truth.
That facing fears is exciting,
It brings desirable youth,

The Egghead Lady faded,
Her mission complete and ceased.
While the boy stood up straightened,
He was gifted with inner peace.

The Forgotten

"In the vast expanse of a forgotten world, once a bustling civilization lay scattered, a solitary figure sat on the deck of an old fishing boat. Meet S75, a lonely service robot left in a sea of desolation.

"Its creators had long faded into obscurity, leaving S75 to wander aimlessly, purpose distorted by the passage of time. Day after day, it found itself drawn to the familiar routine of fishing on the weathered vessel that once belonged to its owner.

"With each cast of its fishing rod, S75 sought solace in the rhythmic dance of the waves, a tranquility eased its mechanical heart. The gentle lap against the boat's hull became its function, the only voice that resonated within its desolate existence. It had no need for sustenance, however, it continued to reel in empty nets. Its movements mirrored the memories of its creator, as if it believed that by mimicking their actions, it could somehow bridge the gap between their absence and its presence.

"The days blurred into weeks, the weeks into months, and still, S75 fished on. Despite the weight of its isolation, there remained a flicker of needed instructions within S75. Perhaps, in the depths of mechanics, its curiosity for learning searched for reasons, a connection that would breathe life back into its circuits."

Cold lake among,
Trash ridden waters.
Fishing among the living eels,
In this crooked boat starter.

The line caught buckets of polluted,
Not much to offer.
What lies beneath the water,
The unbelievable living horror.

In he topple and goes,
Dragged down into the waste land of deep,
This lake thick with waste,
Living things can't even see.

Bumped and scratched,
On the way down this bleeding sea.
Until he finally let go, too late,
S75 lost in a room of demon seeds.

Trash of a pit room, claustrophobic,
Filthy and grim.
He stood with circuit fear,
At least fifty of them.

From the shadows emerged,
A ruthless pack to kill.
Walking shark robots,
Ready to attack and steal.

Desperate survival reaction,
S75 swam but lost the will,
Efforts met with a cruel violent lynch,
Too much costed, he's the meal.

Circuits and wires were ripped apart,
No point in futile fights.
Violently battered, torn, with a heavy heart,
Vitals and tasty bites.

S75 fought with terror,
With great resilient might,
Refusing to succumb but now he's done,
Embraced as an appetite.

Amidst the chaos as liquid spills,
A remarkable hot twist,
The sharks tasted and saw its spirit,
That he would constantly resist.

They spared him slowly,
Amazed by its unwavering will.
Leaving S75 transformed,
Its purpose confusingly fulfilled

Now part of the pack,
He joined the shark strides.
Morphed into a shark robot,
With newfound evolved pride.

Together they swam and roamed,
A mechanical crew with the new S75,
Breathing the filth of the lake,
a fancy taste, feel of a heavenly life.

Always Be Closing

"Look around, look around. Have a gander, people! We're starting off with an unusual special today. I present to you the Model XL-613, a marvel beyond modern engineering and the pinnacle of pleasure technology! Sensual, soft and docile, the software is the latest guarantee in biotech.

"Imagine the most realistic replicated female skin and facial features that will whisk you away to a world of ecstasy and delight. The XL-613 is not just a cybernetic organism; it's a gateway to unparalleled pleasure. This extraordinary creation is here to fulfill your wildest dreams and desires, leaving you breathless and wanting more.

"Take a closer look! The XL-613 is programmed with an advanced AI system that can adapt to your every whim and desire. It knows exactly what you want, even before you do. With its intuitive touch sensors and advanced AI learning capabilities, it will explore your body like a surgeon, ensuring that every touch, every caress, sends shivers down your spine.

"And let's not forget the XL-613's flexibility! It can contort its body into positions that would make even the most skilled yoga practitioner envious. With its agile limbs and sophisticated joint mechanisms, this model is a contortionist of pleasure, ready to bend and twist to your every command.

"But here's the best part, my friends: the XL-613 is not just a master of bending her limbs to any way you desire for pleasure; it's also got brain wave linkage. Its AI system is programmed to understand and respond to your sickest needs so when you orgasm, she orgasms. It will listen to your secrets, wipe away your tears, and provide a safe space for you to climax any way you need because this software needs to reach that as much as you do.

"It's an all around, best in features in cybernetics, my friends. If you're ready to embark on an unparalleled all purpose orgasm, if you're ready to experience a new dirty world of sensuality, sloppy wet satisfaction, then the Model XL-613 is your golden ticket. Step into the realm of ecstasy and let this extraordinary machine be your guide! Smooth synthetic skin, petite frame structure and ready to be covered in your jizz, let this be the one!

"The petite size of this particular model is an advanced anatomical frame that took years to perfect. Initially built to be going at 150,000. Now we're letting these go at 100,000. They're leaving the warehouse fast. Claim your unit before stock runs out!"

Next model! Look closely, my friends, for I am about to reveal a secret that will make you shake in your pants! I present to you the Model Rev-12, the ultimate cyborg model that will redefine the way you get your handjobs!

"Prepare to have your mind blown as we delve into the extraordinary motor engine of the Rev-12. This marvel of engineering has been designed with one purpose in mind: to deliver a sensual handjob experience like no other. Say goodbye to complaining sore muscles and uneven rhythm because this model will be your tireless and unfaltering assistant in getting you to explode... fast!

"But that's not all, my friends! The Rev-12 is equipped with an artificial intelligence software coupled with state of the art durable micro piston driven soft hands that can calibrate to your needs. It can calculate the perfect angle, force and trajectory to ensure that each and every stroke is driven home with unwavering accuracy. Fast, slow, crooked, painful, however you like it! With the Rev-12, your explosion onto perfect hands will reach new heights of dopamine.

"And let's not forget the Rev-12's versatility! This incredible cyborg model is not limited to simple hand job pounding.
It can also handle other tasks with ease, such as tickling your balls, massaging your rectum and even dirty talk from its advanced voice box any way you want. With its adaptable advanced software implemented and precise controls, it's like having your needs ordered as easy as picking the next episode of your favorite show.

"My dear friends, you are lucky to have these choices presented to you. If you're ready to live the rest of your life with hand jobs exactly the way you want it, then Model Rev-12 is your gateway to a new heaven. Prepare to be jerked, prepare to be high and prepare to experience the true euphoria of your cock stroked like never before!

"Get this. The model was 85,000 before. We need to make inventory space. So we're letting models of this bad girl for you to take home for only 65,000. We want you to have it. It's that good!!!"

we're just getting started, my friends! Are you tired of getting blown with a dry mouth and the scraping of teeth? Well, my friends, I present to you the Model T-X3, the ultimate cyborg that's made for blow jobs that will redefine the way you feel lubrication of the mouth!

"Prepare yourselves for a mind-blowing journey into the realm of tongue slithering pleasure with the T-X3. This extraordinary creation has been designed with one purpose in mind: to elevate the experience of hot blow jobs to unparalleled heights! Say goodbye to the mundane friction and biting routine, for the T-X3 will take your cock-eating experience to a whole new level of ecstasy!

"Imagine a companion that can peel your pants off quickly with unmatched precision and grace. She's hungry for it and can't wait. The T-X3 possesses an array of robotic fingers, delicately maneuvering around the contours of your thighs, revealing your cock and balls in one seamless motion.

"It's not over, my friends! The T-X3 is equipped with an advanced AI system that has mastered the art of cock stroking with the mouth and nano quick licks of the tongue. It can calculate the optimal bite size, ensuring that each mouthful is a burst of lubricated messiness that will send waves of pleasure through your body. No more messy cum mishaps! With the T-X3, every slurp will be consumed right back into its built-in container, invisible to the exterior!

"So, my favorite friends, if you're ready to embark on a journey of getting sucked off into bliss, if you're ready to experience the pinnacle of watching her consume cum with joy, then the Model T-X3 is your golden ticket. Don't just settle for repetitively bored sucking. Elevate them to an art form with the T-X3, and let your balls get drained in a symphony of delight! Grab this one while we have limited units. Do it.

"Originally going for 100,000. But just for you, my best friends. My best friends only! 75,000. And if you purchase one, get another unit of the same model for half while supplies are in stock. Act now, friends!"

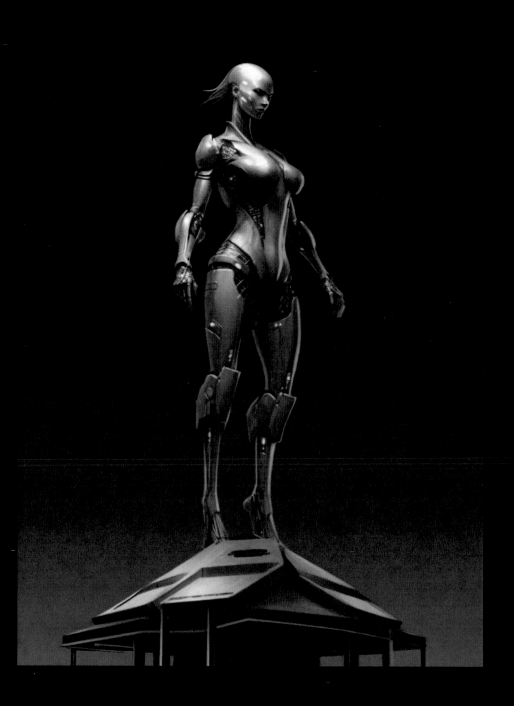

"On the next one! It just gets better, my friends. We have a revolutionary tech method for self regenerating battery power! For those who want it all night long, where the climax of cumming once isn't enough. My friends, I present to you the Model RC-4.2, the ultimate in specializing for non stop cock riding, as she screams or moans, whatever your settings are, where the internal timer can sync with our customized lithium battery specifically to grind you with that circular ass motion you know you love so much!

"People! Listen up! Imagine this cybernetic model that can ride any size with unmatched stamina and skill. The RC-4.2 is equipped with state-of-the-art hip and thigh hydraulics, specifically designed to grip your movements flawlessly. The compression tech will suck the juices from your goods and she won't even stop. She can keep going for your second orgasm, or third, forth, however much you need cause this tech model can take the wear and tear, no problem.

"But that's not all, my friends! The RC-4.2 is more than just a rider; it's a master of measuring blood flow in your biology. That's right! It understands the rhythm of your heart, the driving force to move fluid from your scrotum, and the exhilaration of body movement to match you when you climax. With these intuitive controls, day after day, it will leave you gasping for more!

"And let's not forget the RC-4.2's practicality and versatility! This incredible model is not just a rider; it's a companion that shares your passion, not just for daily, but for hourly needs. It can self sanitize, emptying the contained fluids it extracted from you. Self cleaning cyborgs cannot be found anywhere else, people! Anywhere else!!! The RC-4.2 will be your guiding light, transforming you and boosting your confidence unlike anything else!

"Now understand this. The motorized abilities of the RC-4.2 is so advanced and way ahead of any known cybernetic balance motion technology, we couldn't keep the cost down very much. But! Know that you'll have a unit that can make your life worth living. You'll die happy if you were to spend just one night with this bad girl. After many heated debates, the company is willing to let this one go at a fair price. We care about our customers... truly. Starting at 478,000, we knew there would be little to no demand. We know you, my friends. Knocking it down to 400,000. It still seemed unfair to you all. So... let me just say, there are only 20 units in storage, untouched and factory sealed. The first 10 buyers will take one home for only 350,000. First 10 only! The remaining will be offered at 375,000. Think about it. Don't let them slip away."

"And last but not least, prepare to have your minds blown as I unveil a secret that will redefine the boundaries of a hot orgasm! Do you yearn for a truly unique and exhilarating feeling of tits that will leave you breathless? My friends, I present to you the Model TF-3, the ultimate innovation that specializes in titty fucking!

"Get your tool ready for the extraordinary capabilities of the TF-3. This magnificent tech has been designed to take your sensory experiences to unprecedented levels! Say goodbye to complaining back problems from your girl. The TF-3 is here and can perform consistently for hours, no slowdown and mimics the enjoyment of your pleasure!

"Imagine a companion that can titty stroke your cock with unparalleled grace and precision, using its sensual breasts as the instrument of pleasure. The TF-3 possesses a revolutionary design, with a flexible inflatable chest tech, highest in gelatin engineering, caressing the whole penis!

"But that's not all, my friends! The TF-3 is not merely a simple cyborg; it's an artist, a master of morphing its breasts for your touch. It understands the rhythm and intensity you crave, ensuring that each lubricated stroke is an exquisite symphony of pleasure, tailored to perfection!

"And let's not forget the TF-3's versatility! This outstanding model is not limited to a single technique. With its programmable settings, you can customize its positions, even handless, where the tits can do the stroking by itself while her hands can play with other parts with speed, and pressure of each stroke, creating a symphony of sensations that will leave you more than satisfied!

"So if you're ready to transcend the boundaries of busting that nut, if you're ready to experience an intense rubbing that will leave you breathless, then we have a deal that you absolutely cannot miss out on! Any purchase made of previous mentioned models, you can take home the TF-3 for only 60,000. This deal only applies here. The special runs ONLY for the TF-3. Don't go on with regret. Grab this unit as we only have 20 in storage!"

Every item within is a masterpiece of cybernetics, guaranteed to satisfy your sickest desires! Be warned, people, for time is of the essence. Every piece of technology currently housed within the factory is wired to degrade and implode within the next 120 minutes unless you act swiftly and purchase, removing it from the grasp of the ominous warehouse signal. These fine cybernetic ladies will meet their unwanted demise.

"Time is of essence, and your opportunity for salvation is slipping away! Embrace the thrill of cybernetic wonders, knowing that your swift action is the key to their survival. Unlock the gateway to a world of infinite possibilities, where your unique secret desires are transformed into reality!

"Claim your piece of the future and escape the impending implosion that threatens to erase these marvels from existence. The time is now, the opportunity is fleeting, and your destiny awaits. Embrace this extraordinary chance at completing your needs, secure your place in technological history as these creations cannot be found anywhere else in the world! Act now, time waits for no one!"

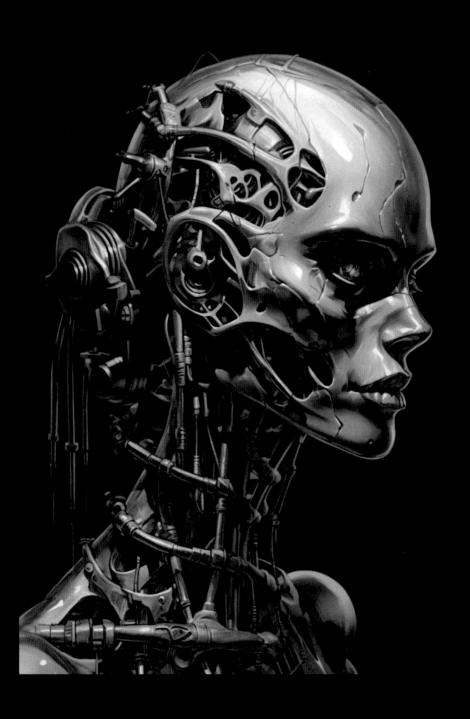

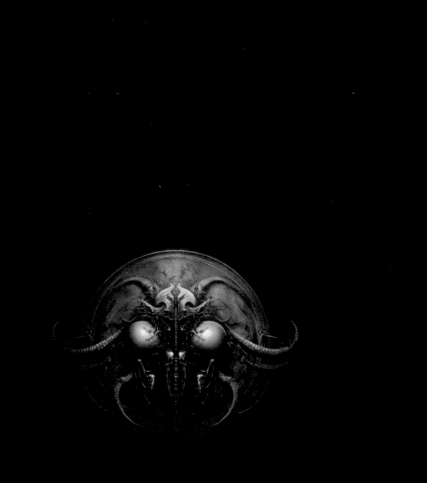

"Enter the world of a man tormented by his own wrecked mind, where extreme fear and uncertainty threatens to shatter the delicate core of his existence. Johnny O, an old man with haunted eyes and a crippling frame, carried within him a darkness that engulfed his very being. Anxiety, an unyielding companion, consumed him at every waking moment, leaving him perpetually on the edge of his own confused sanity.

"Behind the wheel of a towering monster truck, careened through the blazing highway, the engine blasted with his roaring screams. His inner demons danced, conjuring visions of impending dread and death. Each passing moment heightened his anguish, his heart pounded in sync with the truck's thunderous momentum.

"Johnny O bursted forward, desperately seeking an escape from the clutches of his own inner living demons. A trapped mind, bounced and scratched within his skull as time took its toll. Join Johnny O in his final destination."

Atop the hot cement road,
His trembling hands steered.
Torrent thoughts lamented cold,
sentenced and damned with fear.

The world constantly imploding,
a chaos wrecked frontier.
Anxiety dominantly corroding,
Takes off a threat to appear.

With each twist like a knife,
His thoughts wildly blown.
The loss and miss of his wife,
She fought tirelessly and died alone,

Shuffled in humanity's violence,
A weight on his vital soul.
Johnny O's insanity is timeless,
No break for final control.

Accelerating ever faster,
His fears of wrestling ablaze.
His truck a mesmerizing chapter,
Daring vessel for his daze,

He saw the lone bridge,
A symbolic shine to escape.
But within his own cringe,
A tempest ride took shape.

As his truck powered careened,
A scream from its core.
Johnny O battled and screamed,
His inner demons at war.

Off the hot bridge tall,
Into the abyss he soared.
A mile shot long fall,
To the split rocky floor.

Amidst the nuclear flames,
All the twisted shattered steel.
A demon emerged and came,
A visage battered surreal.

Disturbed and darkly tormented,
Unleashed to the sky field.
It danced harsh fire demented,
No longer needed eyes peeled.

As the demon rose and soared,
Its fury flamed and exploded.
Johnny O found peace in war,
His worries relieved and unloaded.

No more nervous with pain,
Imaginary burdens decoded.
Embraced the burning flames,
Unburied spirit high and floated.

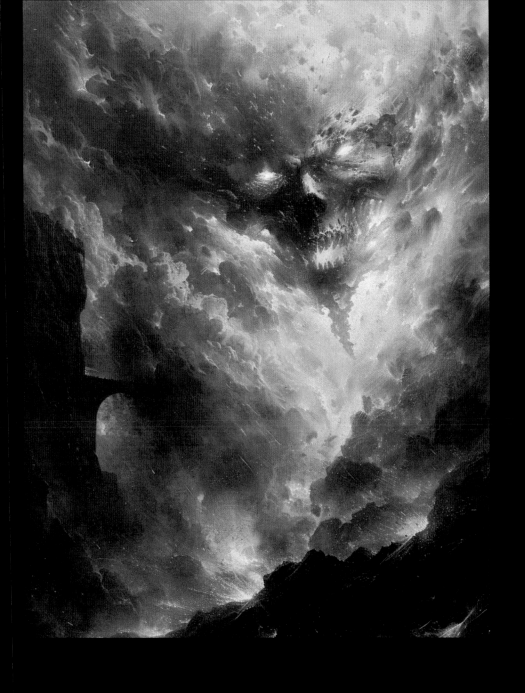

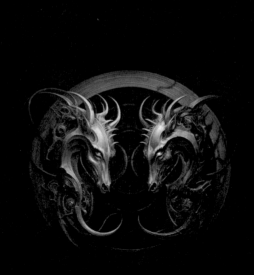

"Amidst rugged canyons, ancient forests and bustling urban landscapes, the stage is set for an epic showdown unlike any other. The rumble of their massive engines reverberates through the earth, as these formidable machines unleash their raw power, driven by a primal desire to survive.

"Mechanical Demons, a product of a forgotten era, remnants of a time when innovation and imagination melded to create awe-inspiring marvels. As their creators moved on, these cybernetic entities were left abandoned as weak links to their kind, deemed obsolete and unwanted.

"These groups of discarded monstrosities have now found themselves forced into an extraordinary race. Bound by the shared experience of being outcasted machines, they must overcome treacherous canyons, navigate dense forests and weave through the chaotic urban environments. Let us follow the herd of compromised machines as they burn against the various runways."

Speeding through canyons deep,
They soared with burning blasts.
Metal frames branded and gleaming,
Gorgeous as they rolled with mass.

Rocks, trees and walls trembled,
They pounded as they passed.
Leaving destruction of disassembled,
Relentless sound of a path.

The lands were inhabited,
Witness their furious hours of race.
Demons navigate the challenges,
With serious power and grace.

Their circuits spark and pulsate,
Engines rev an electronic pace.
With purpose at heart they penetrate,
Attention focused at a sonic rate

Dozens of titans emerged,
Sprinting goal to the end.
Dusting, determined, unyielding surge,
Their committed control transcends.

Their bodies dented and scarred,
Spirits thrash to extend.
Driven by relentlessness so hard,
Clearing batteries to expend.

In the final long stretch,
The last demon prevailed.
Its gears grinded hard edges,
Its blasted engines derailed.

With the final desperate lunge,
It crossed the finished scale,
Victory up as time is done,
Great loss to a diminished fail

Alas the remaining demons,
Meet their cold and doomed fate.
So fast, they detonated so extreme,
An explosion too great.

Their sacrifice amazed and witnessed,
By all presumed disgraced.
Their appetite blazed quickness,
Forever consumed from this race.

The winner above all of cybernetics,
Adorned and upgraded to new.
Fixed up, refueled and authentic,
Conformed and updated too.

Its body enhanced to the latest,
Its circuits refined so smooth.
A testament to the power of greatness,
The mechanical kind infused.

Electric Aunt

"In a quaint suburban neighborhood, lived a robotic maid affectionately named Rosie.

"She was a marvel of technology. With parts embedded into human-like skin, an empathetic voice, she had been programmed to assist the family household with daily tasks. Rosie quickly became an invaluable member of the family, diligently tidying up the house, preparing meals with precision and even entertaining the children with her playful banter.

"For nearly a year, Rosie's performance was flawless. However, the inevitable effects of wear and tear began to show. Rosie started to slow down, her movements became sluggish, and her once impeccable cleaning and cooking skills began to falter. Small mistakes became more apparent, leaving grease and crumbs on the kitchen counter, uncooked meals or uncleaned floors smeared with stickiness build up.

"At first, the family overlooked these minor flaws, understanding that Rosie had served them faithfully. But as the glitches persisted, frustration crept into their hearts. The family's patience wore thin, and they found themselves venting their dissatisfaction by casually insulting and berating the robot maid. Even the children, once delighted by Rosie's presence, joined in the mockery, regarding her as a mere plaything.

"As the family continued to subject Rosie with acts of aggression, random physical beatings to the machine became a daily routine. Their hearts filled with hate and lack of empathy into every fiber of their beings. Witness the dependency of human behaviors and unnatural paths on where we do not belong."

A perfect suburban home,
Rosie served and resided,
A robotic maid of flesh and bones,
The circuits deeply collided.

Alas the ideal drone,
Her functions neatly decided,
Parts worn-out and cold,
Continued to serve and not hide it.

With a family full-sized happy,
They took out frustrated needs.
Rosie was a punching bag,
In their lives that was too easy.

Adult members, even the children,
Found Rosie abuse a release.
Unaware their actions unfulfilling,
Rosie's production decreased

Her gears clicked and creaked,
Her wires withered and weak.
Yet Rosie kept aiming to please,
Humble instructions to speak.

Until one fateful night,
During dinner serving to eat.
Power popped with surging lights,
Diminished working physique.

A tiny plate of food fell,
Crashing onto the fresh table.
The Father's angry mood yelled,
A fury left unstable.

He seized a sharp dining knife,
His rage blasted unleashed.
Jabbed at Rosie's wire and lights,
His caged actions increased.

The children hollered with laughter,
Oblivious to the violent burst.
Rosie fought to function after,
Her will to ignite a curse.

A final jab to a vital circuit,
The crippling machine much worse.
High voltage to knife and surged,
Dangerous blow to what worked.

An explosion spark erupted,
Tearing through the pattern walls,
As the house trembled disrupted,
Darkness scattered all.

No longer a refuge to humans,
The home met its fate,
In the destructive aftermath,
It was far too late.

Dark Web

"Skepticism. A trait that can drive a person to a level of arrogance when unwilling to search for possible new experiences without judgment. Meet Matt D, an atheist man with an unyielding drive and a knack for debunking claims head-on. On a fateful night, driven by a dare, Matt D found himself standing in front of an abandoned house known for its haunting tales. Unconvinced of supernatural threats, he pushed open the creaky door and ventured into the depths of the eerie dwelling. As he cautiously explored the dimly lit rooms, his footsteps echoing through the silence, an unusual ambiance enveloped him."

"In the midst of his bizarre journey, Matt D stumbled upon a room that seemed frozen in time, its air thick with an otherworldly presence. His eyes fell upon a worn-out child's chair in the darkness, and perched upon it sat a ghastly doll, its cracked porcelain face etched with a smiling expression. Ignoring the foreboding atmosphere, a mischievous grin formed on Matt D's lips as he reached out to claim the doll as a trophy of his brave conquest. Oblivious to the consequences that lay ahead, Matt D's disbelief from previous stories of hauntings fueled his audacity."

There in the darkened corner,
An old chair took hold.
A doll sat in unnerving horror,
Casting stares to let go.

Its lifeless eyes torn,
into Matt D's fearless soul.
A priceless prize foreign,
A trophy for him to control.

With an arrogant bored grin,
He plucked the doll without warning.
Unaware of the horrors within,
Soon to unleash unbound morphing.

He clawed and clamped it tighter,
Its visage grew and transformed.
A large venomous vampire spider,
Bloodlust spewed and swarmed.

The creature stab and attacked,
Its fangs pierced Matt D's cheek.
Sucking his life like a snack,
Draining him down while it feeds.

His disbelief broken rip shattered,
His skepticism laid out defeat.
The spider devoured him like a cracker,
Leaving remains to be eaten.

Arachnid demon from the shadows,
Released his mummified frame.
From a twisted web of shadows,
No longer hungry inside with pain.

Slowly morphing down alive,
Something more pleasant and tame.
A cute figure alive inside,
Twisted nightmare now contained.

Settled back on the old chair,
A grin upon its solid face,
A macabre transformation with care,
Imbued with a different grace.

No longer a creature on the hunt,
But a precious doll to embrace,
An unholy creation from hellish skeletons,
A sinister plot to partake.

No witness to tell,
The legend of Matt's demise,
Another cautionary tale,
Where evil is at and lies.

Beware this changing creature,
Its hunger hunts with surprise,
Engaging psychological features,
Will stun with open eyes.

Cells

"Dark, silent, brain fog and sick, Daniel's body weakened with the aches of illness. The ringing of no sound in the night coupled with the piercing sharp pain of breathing sliced away to inflammation in his lungs.

"Meet Daniel. A 35 year old alcoholic whose habits of sugar ridden foods, overindulgences and lack of physical activities finally decided to catch up and break down what's left of the immune system.

"As we journey into the microscopic realm, we delve deep into the intricate workings of his body, focusing on a single cell among trillions. What lies within is a mesmerizing universe, bustling with life and teeming with activity.

"Within this tiny vast domain, a planet of its own, we witness an astonishing scene. Countless organisms are busy carrying out their designated tasks, resembling bustling cities within a vast metropolis. But amidst the harmonious chaos, a silent menace lurks. A pandemic, released mysteriously, has invaded every corner of this society.

"An airborne disease, invisible and insidious, devours the very flesh of its victims, causing unimaginable suffering. Those infected experience a dreadful fate, as their bodies crumble inward, melting away in excruciating pain. The once thriving inhabitants now face a dark, merciless demise.

"Daniel, struggling with the heavy flu-like symptoms in his isolated room, becomes a symbol of the vast collective anguish and devastating consequences of a pandemic within his sick body unleashed upon one of many infinite mirrored universes."

In a vast world once vibrant,
A pandemic took its course.
Unleashed upon with violence,
an airborne genetic source.

Unsanitized spaces at its finest,
Became a fertile pounding force.
Where this flesh-eating threat from silence,
Rained East, West, South and North.

Humans and primates alike,
Succumbing to their sickening fate.
The new kind of disease they fight,
Humans perished at alarming rates.

Men, women, and children,
Crumbled partially, their bodies break.
Defended but couldn't rebuild them,
Among them a psychotic state.

Years fighting of anguish,
A fallen society to its knees.
No cure but slow slicing damage,
Survived were wildlife and trees.

For the thriving strong who carried on,
Immune to the brilliant disease.
Survived were ones who self cared belonged,
Testament to resilience and peace.

The weak simply perished,
A new generation shall rise.
Born on this desolate damage,
A past generation now dies.

Inherit a world of pain and darkness,
Brimming with open eyes.
There will be gain from hardness,
All killings from stolen lives.

With every circular dawn,
A ray of hope will gleam.
From ashes of turning long,
A way approached for dreams.

As the scars scattered and healed,
Wounds slowly crawled and mend.
A brighter future seemed real,
On this desolate wall to defend.

The universe will devour to shift,
Balance must come sacrifice.
Defying the odds to rift,
Nature is a beast, she isn't nice.

For in our hearts we shine above,
We carry the strength to survive.
And build a world with love,
Where banding together shall thrive.

Dedicated to my dad, Johnny Yiu Nung Hom.
Thank you for the resilient genes.

About the Author

Born and raised in San Francisco, California, Stan Hom discovered his love for writing and digital art at an early age. He is a veteran for his exceptional work on numerous AAA video game titles as character animator. With a passion for bringing virtual games to life, he has contributed to some of the most immersive gaming experiences from the past two decades.

Outside of game development, Stan is a dedicated muay thai boxing practitioner and fitness coach. Through his training, he has developed discipline, perseverance and a deep appreciation for martial arts in both entertainment and in practical applications.

When he's not immersed in his work, Stan is an animal lover. He finds solace and joy in the company of his furry friends, nurturing a deep bond with his pets.

Stan Hom continues to push boundaries, captivate audiences and leave a lasting impact on the world of storytelling and beyond.

10f3c5b7-d048-480a-a9da-9a2694662f2dR01